Where is Puka

Julia Gravesmiller

Where is Puka

iUniverse books may be ordered through booksellers or by contacting:

iUniverse
1663 Liberty Drive
Bloomington, IN 47403
www.iuniverse.com
844-349-9409

ISBN: 978-1-6632-2236-7 (sc)
ISBN: 978-1-6632-2237-4 (e)

Library of Congress Control Number: 2021908711

Print information available on the last page.

iUniverse rev. date: 04/29/2021

Introduction

"Where Is Puka" is a story about a magical bear who belongs to a young boy named John. Puka represents a symbol of hope, friendship and support for when kids are experiencing emotions like loneliness, depression, nervousness, and others that they aren't really familiar with and don't know how to deal with them. He's a comforter, friend, and just someone kids trust that they could confide in. In this story, John's mother unfortunately lost Puka at the park, and due to the fact that John had such an attachment to him, he went through a lot of sadness because he lost his best friend until they found Puka again.

Where
is
Puka

It was a beautiful sunny day and John thought to himself "What do I want to do today?" He said "I know I will go to the park. Puka, would you like to go to the park with me?" We will have lots of fun.

"Mom?" Said John,"Can we go to the park today?" "Yes," said mom, "it is a beautiful day to go to the park." John was excited, he ran to get his ball and to get puka.

"John, maybe we should leave Puka here until we get back." Mom said. John said "no I promised Puka we would go to the park and have fun today just me and Puka." "Okay." said mom and off they went to the park.

It was such a nice day that there were so many children playing in the park, everyone must have had the same idea to go to the park. John saw some of his friends in the park and they wanted to play on the sliding board they asked John if he wanted to come and play, and John said yes.

So, john sat puka on the bench next to his mom, his mom was reading a book, and he went to play with his friends.

A woman said "excuse me, can you help me, I am trying to get to the library can you tell me how to get there?" "Sure." said John's mom. She told the woman how to get to the library.

"Thank you so much." said the woman, "You're welcome." said John's mom. She went to sit back down on the bench where puka was sitting, but puka was not there.

While she was giving the woman direction to the library, there was a little boy walking by and saw puka sitting all by himself, so he took puka home with him.

John's mom returns to the bench where puka was sitting and puka was gone. "Oh my!" She yelled "Where is Puka? I left him sitting here I was only gone for a minute." She called out "Puka! Where are you?" but she couldn't find him anywhere.

Where could he have gone? John is going to be so upset. John came over to his mother, "Mom where is Puka?" "John, I have some bad news."

"There was this woman that needed my help finding the library and I took my eyes off puka for only a minute, and when I returned puka was gone."

John started to cry out "Puka! Where are you?" "I must find Puka." Said John, "I must." So, John and his mom looked all over the park, but they could not find Puka. John was so sad he said "I should've left Puka at home, it is all my fault." "No john it is my fault you left him with me, but we will find him I promise. We will go home, and I will make posters and put them around the neighborhood, lost teddy bear name Puka if you find him please call right Away." Mom said. John and his mom did just that.

The next day the little boy that took Puka home saw the poster about the lost bear name puka. He knew that this bear must be incredibly special to the owner of the bear. He told his mom and his mom called the number, "Are you looking for a bear a stuffed bear?

My son found a stuffed bear in the park yesterday sitting on a bench and there was no one sitting with him so he bought the bear home with him."

"Yes, he was sitting on the bench alone for a few minutes while I helped a woman that was lost, and when I came back puka was gone." Mom said. "Well you can come to my house and see if this is your bear Puka." The woman said. "Thank you very much, we will be right over."

John and his mom arrived at the little boy house; his mom answered the door. "Hello, my name is Angela, this is my son John." "Hi, my name is Julia, and this my son Joseph.

Joseph go to your room and bring the stuffed bear out." When Joseph came out the room John was so excited "Puka, mom it's Puka! Thank you, yelled John."

Joseph was sad but he knew it was not his bear to keep. John and his mom took Puka home. John's mom thought about Joseph and how sad he looked when they took Puka home.

She went to the toy store and bought a big stuffed bear and she and John took it to Joseph's house and gave it to Joseph, he was so happy he has a big stuffed bear of his own. John and his mom went home.

The End

Printed in the United States
by Baker & Taylor Publisher Services